Tales of Lake Superior

A grandmother's stories of the north

by

Juliet Beatrice Lind

Book Design and Illustrations by Joan Henrik

*This book is dedicated to
Grandmothers everywhere who have shared their love
of the earth and its many mysteries
with their grandchildren. These women have inspired
this series of stories. In particular,
Grandmother Ruby"Rockhound" Swenson Niemi,
who spent her whole life around Lake Superior
and wanted to share her love of the lake with her family.
Many of these stories include factual events that occurred
with one of her twenty grandchildren and
twenty-six great-grandchildren.*

Smelting

Jonny Lump-Lump had come to visit his grandmother.

This was the first time he had come to stay without his mother and father, and he was very excited. Jonny's grandmother lived on the shores of Lake Superior. Jonny Lump-Lump always said that Lake Superior was the biggest lake in the world! Jonny was right. Lake Superior is the largest fresh-water lake in the world.

Grandmother often explained, "The oceans are bigger but ocean water is salty and you can't drink it."

"I can drink all the water I want from Lake Superior, can't I Grandmother?" Jonny asked.

"That's right," she smiled. "Would you like a glass of water, Jonny?"

As Jonny sipped the cold water he thought it was the best tasting water he had ever tasted.

Jonny Lump-Lump loved to visit his grandmother. They often walked along the shore of Lake Superior. His grandmother would tell him stories about the native people who lived by the lake when her parents had come from the "old country," and she would tell him stories about the boats from far away places that sailed on the lake.

Grandmother would make-up stories about the things they found on the beach. They found interesting pieces of driftwood, glass, colorful rocks, and many other things. If the treasures they found were not too big, Jonny stuffed the new found treasures in his pocket until his pockets stuck out like two big lumps on either side of the pant legs. One day his grandmother started to call him Jonny Lump-Lump and that is how he got his nickname. From that time on his grandmother always called him Jonny Lump-Lump. He liked his nickname because it is what his grandmother had nicknamed him, and that made it special.

But of all the things Jonny Lump-Lump liked, Grandmother's stories were the best.

"Now it is springtime, and this is the very best time to walk along the shore of Lake Superior," Grandmother explained as he was getting ready for bed.

"Tomorrow we will find many treasures on the beach. These treasures are left on the beach by the winter storms," she explained.

Early the next morning Grandmother made French toast with fresh maple syrup. Grandmother's friend tapped his maple trees every spring and collected the syrup, just as the native people did years ago. Then he cooked it to make it thick and sweet. It was so tasty.

"Why don't you put on that yellow plastic raincoat and those rubber boots," Grandmother suggested. "They will help keep you warm and dry while we walk the beach."

Jonny and Grandmother walked hand-in-hand down to the beach.

Right away they found a small beautiful rock with different lines of color in it. She said the rock was called an agate. Next, they found a big piece of driftwood that looked like an alligator.

Jonny climbed onto the driftwood and yelled, "Gittee-up Gittee-up", swinging his arms over his head, acting like a cowboy riding a horse.

Jonny jumped off the driftwood and ran to the edge of the lake to look into the water. Just then, he saw a silver flash go through the water. "Grandmother! Come here!" Jonny yelled. "Look, look in the water!"

"What did you see, Jonny?" Grandmother asked.

Jonny told his grandmother about the silver flash he had seen in the water. Just as he pointed to the spot where he had seen it, the silver flash was there again.

Suddenly there were many silver flashes in the water. "What is it, Grandmother?" Jonny asked.

Grandmother put her hands on Jonny's shoulders and told him it was smelting time again. "Every year at this time a small fish called a smelt come close along the shore of the lake, Jonny. The small rainbow smelt are going up the rivers to lay their eggs.

There were no smelt in Lake Superior when my parents came from the 'old country'," Grandmother said. "The smelt came into the lake from the other Great Lakes. That was just about the time your mother was born. Your mother loved to fish for the smelt when she was a young girl. She thought it was best to go smelting at night and build a fire on the shore of Lake Superior."

Grandmother thought Jonny could catch some smelt that afternoon. After lunch she found an old pair of high boots, a kitchen strainer, and an empty coffee can. She told Jonny he would need these things if he wanted to go smelting. "You will need the high boots so you can walk into the lake to catch the smelt, Jonny," Grandmother explained. "You will catch the fish in the strainer, not with a fishing pole and hook, because the smelt are so small. When you catch some smelt, you put the smelt in the coffee can to carry them home," Grandmother laughed.

Jonny Lump-Lump and Grandmother hurried down to the shore of the lake. Jonny slowly moved into the lake. Step-by-step, he moved into the deeper water. Jonny dipped the strainer into the water. Slowly, he lifted the strainer out of the water. In the strainer jumped three small, silver fish!

Jonny ran out of the water to his grandmother. "Grandmother!" Jonny yelled; "Look what I caught!"

"Jonny Lump-Lump, you are now the family fisherman," Grandmother laughed. "Tonight we will eat smelt for dinner."

"Jonny," Grandmother said at dinner, "you must remember to take only as many smelts as we can eat. We don't want to waste any of the smelt. We don't want to waste anything."

Every day for the next week Jonny fished for smelt. He and Grandmother ate the wonderful tasting fish every day. Jonny gave smelt to the neighbors all around Grandmother's house.

"I think we've eaten enough smelt, Jonny," Grandmother said one morning. But Jonny wanted to go smelting again.

Jonny told his grandmother he was going to go out and play while she cleaned the house. When Jonny reached the back door, he grabbed the strainer out of the coffee can and hid it under his raincoat. He ran out the back door and down to the beach. He dipped his strainer into the water and caught ten small smelt right away. Jonny dumped the jumping fish on the sand. He watched the smelt flip and flop on the sand. After a few minutes the smelt all lay still. Quickly, Jonny threw one into the water. But the smelt floated on top of the water and the waves pushed the fish back to shore.

Jonny ran across the sand. He found a spot high on the beach and dug a hole. He ran back to where he had left the smelt. He sadly picked up the smelt and walked back to the hole he had dug. He put the smelt in the hole and covered the smelt with the sand.

The next morning Grandmother asked Jonny if he would like to catch smelt to take home to his mother. Jonny thought that was a great idea. They walked to Lake Superior together. Jonny looked at the spot where he had hidden the smelt, feeling sad and guilty.

Quickly, Jonny Lump-Lump walked into the water. He dipped the strainer and raised it slowly out of the water. But – no fish flipped in the strainer. Again and again he tried, but no smelt were in the lake.

Jonny walked slowly out of the water. He put his arms around grandmother and started to cry. "Oh, Grandmother it is all my fault! I did a bad thing. You told me not to waste the smelt but I did. Now, they're all gone!"

'What have you done, Jonny?" Grandmother asked.

Jonny took Grandmother's hand and walked up the beach to where he had hidden the smelt. He dug carefully into the sand and uncovered the ten smelt.

Grandmother put her arms around Jonny and he cried on her shoulder.

Later, Grandmother told Jonny to pick up the smelt and put them in the coffee can. She told him they would put one smelt under each of her tomato plants to help them grow. "That way the smelt will not be wasted, after all, Jonny." She said.

After they put the smelt under the tomato plants, Grandmother told Jonny, "The smelt run is over for this year Jonny; that is why there are no fish in the lake. They will be back again next spring. They will again swim up the rivers to lay their eggs."

The next morning Jonny took the bus back home. Slowly the bus went up the hill away from Grandmother's home. As Jonny looked back at Lake Superior he made a promise: He would remember what his Grandmother had warned him about.

It is important never to waste anything.

The Agate

Jonny Lump-Lump looked out the window.

The bus rounded the top of the hill overlooking Lake Superior, Using his jacket sleeve he rubbed the moisture off the window so he could see the lake more clearly. A treasure hunt, he thought, this is what his grandmother had promised him on his last visit.

When Grandmother drove him to the bus station after his last visit she promised, "The very first morning after you arrive I will take you to my favorite treasure hunting spot on Lake Superior. A place where I found some of my most precious treasures."

When the bus arrived at the station, Grandmother was there with open arms to welcome Jonny Lump-Lump.

"Are you ready to go on the treasure hunt I promised, Jonny?" She asked.

"Oh, yes Grandmother, I can't wait!" He smiled up at her.

"When we get home I will show you what kind of treasures we will be looking for, Jonny," Grandmother explained.

When they reached Grandmother's home on the shore of Lake Superior they carried his suitcase up the steps into the house.

"Jonny, come into my bedroom. I want to show you something." As they walked into her bedroom Jonny noticed a small table next to the bed that he had never seen before.

"This is my new treasure table, Jonny. My friend made this for me. I can lift the top and put my treasures inside and with the glass top I can see what I have stored in it and keep them safe."

Inside the new bedside treasure table were all of Grandmother's precious treasures.

"This is my agate collection Jonny, and I am very proud of them," Grandmother smiled.

She had many, many agates of all sizes, shapes, and colors stored in the treasure table. Grandmother carefully lifted the glass lid and picked out one of the rocks and put it into Jonny's hand. This rock was about the size of a small marble, but it was covered with lines in a circle of many colors. "This is called an eye agate."

"Wow!" Jonny exclaimed. "These agates are really different."

"These are my most precious treasures. I have collected agates for many years, Jonny," Grandmother explained. "It is very difficult to find really good stones now; there are lots of people who like to hunt for them. The most difficult agates to find are big ones with lots of lines and bright colors.

Jonny and his grandmother stood over the table for a long time, looking at each and every agate in Grandmother's new treasure table.

Right after breakfast the next morning, Jonny and Grandmother drove to Agate Beach on the north shore of Lake Superior. They walked hand-in-hand down to the rocky shore of the lake.

"This beach is sure different than the beach by your house Grandmother." Jonny remarked.

"That's why it is a great place to find agates, Jonny. The water has carried the rocks and dumped them here on the shoreline. Now we can start the treasure hunt. We have lots to choose from, but it takes a special eye to be a good agate hunter. My mother would call me 'Eagle Eye' when we used to hunt for agates because I could spot them so quickly. But, now it takes careful searching and patience.

"We are looking for all different kinds of agates and they are hard to find because agates crack easily and break into small pieces.

The agates we want to find will have lots of lines and circles of color all through the rock. I think they are beautiful."

"It would be easier if we had a treasure map, right Grandmother? Jonny laughed.

Jonny Lump-Lump and Grandmother walked the beach for a long time and found driftwood, floats from a fishing net, and even an old green bottle with a cork in it, and rocks, lots and lots of rocks. But, they found no agates.

The north shore of Lake Superior was covered with rocks and huge boulders. Jonny climbed on top of one big boulder and looked out at the white-capped lake.

"Look how mad the lake looks! It is pounding the rocks on the shoreline, Grandmother!" Jonny shouted over the roar of the water.

Grandmother thought it was time they had some lunch, so they set up a picnic on top of a big boulder and ate their sandwiches.

Jonny threw small pebbles into the lake while he was eating.

"How come the rocks are so smooth and round, Grandmother?" he asked.

"The lake washes the rocks in and out as the waves move back and forth, Jonny," Grandmother explained. "The rocks rub against one another and this makes each rock round and smooth; sometime the rocks look as if they have been polished. Why don't you throw some of those bigger stones back into the lake and let them have a chance of getting a better polish, Jonny," Grandmother suggested laughing.

Quickly, Jonny jumped off the big boulder they were sitting on, and landed in a huge pile of baseball sized rocks. He threw rock after rock until he suddenly stopped and said, "Boy, this one is sure different, Grandmother. Take a look at this one."

Jonny held up the rock and said. "It sure is heavy and it is not smooth on the outside like the others."

Jonny handed up a heavy oval rock to his Grandmother. It was different from most of the rocks on the shore because it was pitted on the outside and a grayish-red color. When she turned the rock over in her hand she and Jonny Lump-Lump both gasped, "Oh!" On the flat side of the agate was a rainbow of bright colors and right in the middle was a round eye of color.

Both Grandmother and Jonny smiled. This looks like a real treasure, doesn't it Grandmother?" Jonny asked.

"Yes, Jonny, this rock is an agate, but I think a very special agate. I have a friend who knows all about agates who works at the university. Tomorrow we will go and see him and find out all about your agate. Would you like that, Jonny?" She asked.

Grandmother's friend was an agate expert. He showed Jonny some of the very special agates he had in his rock museum.

But Jonny thought his agate was the biggest and most beautiful agate of all.

"You have found a very rare agate, Jonny. These agates were made over fifty million years ago from iron ore and other minerals. The earth pressed and heated these things to make the beautiful agates. Yours is a perfect specimen because it is so large and has no cracks. Also, Jonny, it is very rare to find an agate with so many lines and circles of color in one stone. This is a perfect museum agate. Would you like to leave it with us to put in a case for many people to see and enjoy?" He asked

After a moment Jonny Lump-Lump held out his hand, giving away his treasured agate.

When Jonny and Grandmother got into the car Jonny began to cry.

"I know I will never find another agate like that one; I just know I won't!" He wailed. "I want to keep it just for myself. I don't care about other people!" Grandmother took Jonny's hand in hers and held it all the way back to Grandmother's home. They drove in silence.

A few days later Grandmother said, "Let's go see your agate, Jonny." When Grandmother and Jonny entered the area where the agates were displayed they saw a group of children standing around a large glass case. Jonny heard a boy say,

"Boy, look at that beauty! If I found that I would never give it up!"

In the middle of the glass case under a spotlight was Jonny Lump-Lump's treasure. A sign next to the agate read:

LAKE SUPERIOR AGATE

Rare in Color, Size, Shape and Quality

Found by and on-loan from Jonny Lump-Lump

Jonny smiled shyly at his grandmother and said, "Now I understand, Grandmother. If you have something special, it is more fun to share it."

"You understand that you can take your agate back whenever you want. Jonny," Grandmother explained.

"Oh, I couldn't do that now, Grandmother. Some kids might come here and they would miss seeing my agate," Jonny said taking his grandmother's hand.

"That's right, Jonny," Grandmother answered smiling at him.

That vacation Grandmother and Jonny Lump-Lump spent a lot of time hunting for agates, and before he went home he had a shoebox full of agates and other treasures, including a photograph of his treasured agate at the museum.

Winter's Story

"I can't wait!" Jonny Lump-Lump thought. "I can't!"

Just then he could feel the bus slow down and turn sharply to the left. Jonny wanted to jump up and yell, "Hooray! We're here!"

Quickly he put his face against the window of the bus. Then he placed his hands on each side of his face to block out the light. Out the window he could see the lights of the town below. He saw that the road, the trees, and the homes were all covered with white snow. It looked like a thick layer of white frosting Grandmother put on her lemon cake.

The lights of the town winked at Jonny. At the bottom of the hill, past the town, lay the lake. Stretching away as far as Jonny could see was Lake Superior. The moonlight made a long, wide silver path on the frozen lake.

Just then the bus made a wide turn and stopped. Jonny Lump-Lump had come to visit his grandmother on Lake Superior for his winter school vacation. He saw her the minute he stepped off the bus. She was waiting with her arms spread wide, standing in the bus depot. "I'm so happy you're here," she whispered in his ear as she hugged him.

When they reached Grandmother's house Jonny let out a whoop.

"Oh, Grandmother," Jonny yelled, "I'm so glad to be here! Let's go down to the lake and find some treasures in the moonlight like we do in the summer," he suggested.

"It's winter, Jonny," Grandmother warned.

"I don't walk the beach at night in the winter because it's cold and dangerous."

"Well then, I hate winter!" Jonny declared, stamping his foot on the snowy ground.

"You hate winter?" Grandmother asked.

"You don't know the story about winter, Jonny," she continued.

"We should not hate things unless we try to understand them first."

Jonny felt better because he knew his grandmother would soon tell him another one of her wonderful stories.

"Come on, Grandmother, let's go inside. It is really cold and windy out here by the lake," Jonny said as he shivered.

Together they carried Jonny's suitcase up the steps and into grandmother's warm, cozy house.

After eating his favorite dinner, Grandmother put a log in the fireplace. Grandmother always served him his favorite meal to eat the first night he came to visit. Afterward, she sat down in her favorite, big, soft chair that was in front of the fireplace and looked out at Lake Superior.

"Come here, Jonny, and I'll tell you Winter's story."

Jonny snuggled into the couch across from Grandmother's chair, holding a big mug of hot cocoa. He was wrapped in a big, brightly colored afghan blanket so only his face could be seen.

And she started her story:

"A long, long time ago, right here by the lake, a woman gave birth. It was an unusual event because the woman gave birth to four beautiful daughters. Their mother named one Spring because she was a lovely pink-faced, happy baby. She named the second baby, Summer, because she had the most beautiful eyes. Her eyes were like big pools of clear water, as blue as the sky. The third baby she named Autumn. She had bright red hair and green eyes and loved to laugh.

The fourth child was different from her sisters. She had very pale skin and was so quiet. She never laughed or cried.

Four Sisters

As the girls grew, Spring, Summer, and Autumn loved to run and jump and play together. They also loved to play with all the animals that lived around the lake.

They laughed at the insects, and tried to sing like the birds. They would listen to the running water in the creeks and rivers and smell the flowers. They loved to float on the lake.

Everything made the three girls so happy that mother wanted them to have everything they loved. Their mother gave them more and more things they could enjoy. As the world became filled with all the things they loved, they grew louder and stronger.

At the same time, the mother noticed that while the other three girls were growing stronger Winter grew weaker and paler.

Winter didn't like the things that the other three girls liked.

This made their mother very sad. She asked Winter what she could do to make her happy. Winter said that all she wanted was a little quiet "once-in-a-while."

Her mother thought about this for a long, long time. Finally, she decided that it was good for everything to have a rest and be quiet.

Slowly, their mother prepared the animals, and the birds, and the insects, and the plants for their rest.

She taught the animals how to store the food they would need for their long sleep. They would hibernate during Winter's time.

Some of the birds would fly south and stay in a warmer place for the resting time. The trees and plants had to prepare for this new time also. They had to store food to survive and they slowly turned different colors. Their leaves turned from green to gold and orange and red and yellow. Autumn thought the leaves turning color was the most beautiful thing she had ever seen. Seeing the leaves in full color next to the blue water of Lake Superior was amazing.

Spring and Summer did not understand what was happening and they began to cry.

But, slowly, Winter grew stronger and that made her mother happy.

The air grew colder and colder everyday. Spring and Summer's tears turned into snowflakes, which all the girls thought were very beautiful. Each snowflake was different from the other snowflakes.

Winter would walk along the lake, enjoying the quiet, growing stronger and more beautiful every day. Her hair seemed blacker and her eyes grew shinier and grayer.

The frozen lake was a mirror in which Winter could see herself.

Time passed and her mother began to worry that Winter looked at herself in the frozen lake too often.

One morning Mother called the four girls to her and told them that they must learn to share the world they lived in and that they couldn't have all they each wanted all the time.

"Sometimes," she told them, "you must think of what is good and pleases others and not just yourself."

But Mother really wasn't fair because she loved to hear laughter and see things growing and having fun, just like her three daughters.

"That is why Winter's time is shorter than Spring's or Summer's or Autumn's, Jonny." Grandmother explained.

"So you see, Jonny," Grandmother smiled, "now you know why you shouldn't hate winter. Tomorrow we will go out on the lake and see if we can see ourselves in the lake mirror and slide on our boots. I think it will be a lot of fun, don't you?" she asked.

"Yes, Grandmother that will be fun," Jonny Lump-Lump smiled. "I think I'll go to bed now. Winter does make you want to rest."

Fog

Jonny Lump-Lump loved Lake Superior.

He enjoyed visiting his grandmother who lived on the shore of the lake. Summer was nearly over and soon he would return home to go back to school.

Jonny and Grandmother had walked the shore almost every day. Jonny loved the feel of the sand under his bare feet as he walked the beach. He loved the sounds of the waves as they rolled and crashed against the shore, and the feel of the wind as it blew against his face. They both enjoyed watching the sea gulls float above the lake looking for fish to eat. But most of all, Jonny loved the fog. As the evenings grew cooler and the wind swept over the warmed water, the fog was created.

Grandmother called foggy days, pea soup days. When they looked out the window it was just like looking into a bowl of pea soup.

Jonny woke to a loud sound, "Oh-OOOOOO, Oh-OOOOOO.

He knew that sound was the foghorn calling. The foghorn was calling to the ships and boats on Lake Superior. The sound would help them find their way in the thick fog and warn them that land was close. It would warn them to watch out or they could run the ship ashore or hit rocks.

"Oh-OOOOOO, Oh-OOOOOO," Jonny called as he ran into the kitchen where Grandmother was making breakfast.

"Oh-OOOOOO, Oh-OOOOOO," Jonny called again. "It's a foggy surprise day today, Grandmother. OH-OOOOO, OH-OOOOOO."

"Why do you call this a surprise day, Jonny?" Grandmother asked

"Because foggy days are always full of surprises. Don't you remember that last foggy day when you and I walked down to the shore and every step was a surprise? We couldn't see what was right in front of us. It was so much fun. Do you remember the giant snake we found on the beach? We didn't see it at all until we almost stepped on it."

"Oh, yes, Jonny, I remember the big ship's rope that had floated to shore and looked just like a giant snake lying on the sand."

Grandmother laughed.

'That rope was as big around as my arm and as long as a train, wasn't it Grandmother?" Jonny asked.

"Yes Jonny, it was a huge rope. Do you know where that rope is now?" Grandmother asked. "It is my fence around my flower garden."

Jonny ran out the door and he stood on the porch and looked at his grandmother's flower garden. All around the flowerbed stretched the snake rope. The rope was nailed on top of wooden stakes that stuck out of the ground. The snake rope was draped from one wooden stake to the next, creating a fence around the garden.

"What a great idea, Grandmother," Jonny said as he walked back into the kitchen.

As Jonny and Grandmother sat down to eat her famous silver dollar pancakes with blueberry sauce on top, she said, "Did you know that it was a foggy day like this when your grandfather died, Jonny?"

"Your grandfather was a fisherman here on Lake Superior, just like my father was. He would catch lake trout and other fish with huge nets and sell the fish to fish companies. The fish companies would sell the fish they caught all over the world. Your grandfather loved and respected Lake Superior. Everyday he would either go fishing – if the weather was good – or on days when the weather was bad he would fix his boat or repair the nets. It was hard work, but Grandfather was happy with his life.

"On the days your grandfather would go fishing, he would get up very early. The day he died it was clear and sunny in the morning. By early afternoon he was far out on the lake and he and his partner had caught lots of fish. The fog came creeping across the water and wrapped around the boat.

Your grandfather couldn't see as far as the end of the boat.

Quickly, the wind grew stronger and the waves grew higher and higher."

"Grandfather did not have a radio on his boat to call for help, but he did have a compass. He knew the directions N, for north, S for south, E for east, and W for west. So, he watched the compass and went in a straight line following the direction that would take him toward shore. He moved along very slowly. When he was four miles from shore he could hear the fog horn calling and he knew he was near land. So, carefully he followed the sound. Sound travels a long way over water, Jonny. But suddenly, he couldn't hear the fog horn, even though the compass still pointed in the same direction.

"Grandfather traveled more and more slowly but suddenly the boat hit against something hard. The waves pushed the boat against the hard thing again and again. Grandfather had hit a huge boulder that was under the water. The boulder cut open the boat like a knife. The boat was filled with fish and was very heavy and low in the water; so, quickly the boat began to sink. Your grandfather's partner was picked up by a huge wave and thrown into the water. He was lucky!

He was holding onto a wooden lid that had covered the fish that were stored in the bottom of the boat. He rode the wooden cover to shore and this saved his life. The cold water in Lake Superior will chill a person so fast that people die in just a few minutes. Your grandfather was trying to save his boat and wasn't able to. He went down with the boat." Grandmother ended her story.

'"Why didn't he hear the fog horn anymore?" Jonny asked sadly

"Well, Jonny Lake Superior has many small and large bays with high bluffs. The rock bluffs block out the fog horn sound. That is why your grandfather couldn't hear the sound anymore.

He was only a short distance from safety. The compass had led him in the right direction, but sometimes there are dangers we can't see. You can't always protect yourself from the dangers you are not aware of Jonny, like the rocks under the water. Your grandfather was a good fisherman and he did everything he could to save himself, but he couldn't see the rocks and he didn't have a radio.

"That is the reason I love to be close to Lake Superior, Jonny. I feel close to your grandfather," she explained.

And on foggy days when the horn blows, it reminds me of your grandfather."

"That makes me sad. Doesn't it make you sad, Grandmother?" Jonny asked.

"Oh, no Jonny, when the foghorn blows, I think of Grandfather and of all the wonderful years we had together and that makes me happy.

"OH-OOOOOO, OH-OOOOOO," the foghorn blew, and Grandmother and Jonny smiled at each other.

The Loons

Jonny Lump-Lump wondered what would happen next.

Jonny Lump-Lump had been staying with his grandmother on Lake Superior for over two weeks. They had walked the shore of Lake Superior every day, finding interesting rocks, pieces of driftwood, and many other treasures. That morning at breakfast Grandmother said to Jonny, "I think we need a change. Let's go on an adventure and visit one of the many beautiful lakes in this area."

As Jonny and Grandmother were driving down the road to the lake, Grandmother explained, "Thousands and thousands of years ago it was much colder here near Lake Superior. Ice and snow covered the ground all year round. The layers of snow and ice were called glaciers. As the glaciers grew larger and heavier, Jonny, they dug huge holes in the earth like a big bulldozer. After many, many years the weather grew warmer and the glaciers started to melt. The melting water from the glaciers ran into the huge holes and filled them up with water. That is why there are hundreds and hundreds of lakes all around Lake Superior."

"And Lake Superior is the biggest lake of all," Jonny said.

"That's right, Jonny," Grandmother smiled

After thinking for a little while, Jonny said, "It's like Lake Superior is the mother and the smaller lakes are all her children. Maybe we should call the lake Mother Superior." They both laughed.

Jonny saw a big white sign by a lake that read,

"Oh! Grandmother could we rent a boat, please?" he asked.

"I think that would be a fine idea," Grandmother agreed.

After they swam in the lake and ate their picnic lunch, Grandmother rented a boat. Jonny and Grandmother carefully put on their life jackets. They checked to make sure the straps were tightly tied. Then, they sat side-by-side on the middle bench of the boat. Grandmother and Jonny started to row out into the lake. Grandmother pulled on her oar and at the same time Jonny pulled on his oar. Before they knew it, they were in the middle of the lake.

"What a wonderful day," Jonny said to his grandmother. "Thank you for renting this boat."

Suddenly, out of the silence came a sound so loud they both stopped rowing.

      OH-OOOO-WOO
        OH-OOOOO-WOO

The sound came again.

      OH-OOOO-WOO
        OH-OOOOO-WOO

They both sat looking out at the lake and looked at each other, not saying a word.

Then Jonny whispered, "Somebody is hurt and needs help."

"Jonny, look over to where I am pointing near the shore," Jonny looked as Grandmother pointed. "Can you see the two large black birds with the white spots?" she asked.

OH-OOOO-WOO
OH-OOOOO-WOO

And the sound came again even louder.

Jonny looked carefully to where his grandmother was pointing.

"Yes, Grandmother! I see something in the weeds by the shore. They are big beautiful birds!"

"Yes, Jonny, they are handsome looking birds. They are called loons. Look carefully and you will see the baby chicks. They are a different color than the parents. The chicks are a soft brown color and they have no spots. Can you see them?" Grandmother asked quietly.

For a few minutes Jonny searched the shore and looked as carefully as he could. Finally, he raised his hand and pointed to a clump of reeds by the shore. "There they are! I found them," he whispered.

"Jonny," Grandmother explained, "loons make their nests in the reeds by the shore to try and keep the chicks safe. The sounds we heard were the parents warning the chicks that danger was near."

"Yes, but why do they sound so unhappy, Grandmother?" Jonny asked.

"I have heard many stories about the loons, but the one story I thought was very interesting was a very old story.

"In the story, one day the loon realized that the reflection on the lake is his own reflection. And he fell in love with himself. After he met his mate and told her about her reflection in the lake, she also fell in love with her own reflection. They didn't want any other loons on their lake. They only wanted to look at their own reflection and no other loons were allowed on their lake. Soon two baby chicks were born. The parents taught their chicks everything they had to learn in four months. Just as soon as the young ones were old enough to fly, they all flew south and spent the cold winter in the warm area learning how to take care of themselves.

" When the parents returned to their lake, the chicks needed to find another lake to live on, because the young loons were just like their parents. They didn't want to see any other loon's reflection in their lake either.

"There used to be loons on all the lakes around North America, Jonny, but people have frightened them away."

"But why do they sound so sad?" Jonny asked again.

"Well, Jonny," Grandmother continued, "maybe the lonely loons soon realized that they would never see their children or grandchildren or their great-grandchildren and this made the loons very unhappy.

"The wail we just heard is the loon calling to the chicks. But, they have many different calls. Some are warnings; some are just letting each other know where they are on the lake. Each loon has its own call, Jonny, so the parents and chicks can recognize each other's calls even after many years.

"But, every time they call, you can hear the sadness in their voice. They know soon the chicks will leave and they will be alone."

"What if you thought you were so beautiful you would never spend time with me or let me come and stay with you," Jonny said. "That would be terrible."

"Yes, Jonny, and how would I see the world through your young eyes if I didn't spend time with you? That really would be terrible! If the old story is true, the loon has paid a terrible price for loving it's self too much."

Jonny stretched out his neck like the loon, and wailed,

OH-OOOO-WOO
OH-OOOOO-WOO

And the loon replied.

The Fire

Jonny Lump-Lump was just finishing breakfast.

He and his grandmother sat at the small round table in front of the window so they could look out at Lake Superior. They watched as the huge ore boat got smaller and smaller as it moved far out onto the lake.

"The boats are loaded with iron ore here and then the iron ore is carried to the steel plants. Some big steel company will heat the iron ore until it is red hot and liquid," she explained. "They will make all kinds of things from the iron ore like nails, trucks and cars, refrigerators and stoves – hundreds of things that people need."

"Oh, and that reminds me, Jonny," she said, "my kitchen needs something also."

"What's that, Grandmother?" Jonny asked.

"Blueberries," Grandmother laughed, "This morning I used the last of the blueberries I had picked and frozen last summer."

"Where do you get the blueberries?" he asked.

"The blueberries grow all around the Lake Superior region, Jonny. I have a favorite berry picking place which is my secret.

Would you like to take a ride and see if the berries are in blossom?" she asked.

"Great, Grandmother!" Jonny shouted as he jumped up from the table and ran for his jacket. "Let's go to your secret place."

"Wait a minute, Jonny," Grandmother called after him. "We have to clean up the kitchen and put the food away first.

I think we should take along a picnic lunch."

As soon as they packed the picnic lunch and cleaned up the kitchen they jumped into Grandmother's car and drove away from Lake Superior into the forest. The trees had new green leaves and the big old pine trees stood tall and straight, their branches thick with evergreen needles. "Look carefully at the side of the road; we may see some animals. Maybe we will see a baby deer if we are lucky," Grandmother said. As they drove farther and farther away from Lake Superior, the road began to twist and curve. They went around a big bend in the road and Jonny yelled, "What happened, Grandmother? Where did all the trees go?"

"This area had a terrible forest fire three years ago, Jonny. This is what happens when a forest burns down. It takes years and years before the forest will look right again," she explained.

"Why would you come here to look for the blueberries?" Jonny asked, confused.

"Nature works in very strange ways sometimes, Jonny. We will drive down this sand road and I will show you my very favorite secret place." She turned onto a narrow sand road that led through a few old burned trees and small green bushes. They went bumping down the sandy road and both Grand-mother and Jonny laughed. Grandmother slowed the car down as they climbed over a small rise in the road and she turned the car sharply left, and stopped.

"The is my secret blueberry picking place, Jonny." Grandmother smiled and pointed out the window. There below the car was a wide field covered with low green bushes. And, right in the middle of the field stood one tree. The tallest pine tree Jonny had ever seen. It had no needles, no bark, and only a few broken branches at the top of the tree.

Boy, is that ever a strange looking tree," commented Jonny. "It looks like it is wearing a hat."

"I think we should have our picnic lunch now, Jonny, and I will tell you all about this tree, the blueberries, and the fire. How does that sound?" she asked.

"Great! I'm getting hungry." Jonny opened the car door and picked up the picnic basket and carried it to the foot of the tree where Grandmother was spreading a blanket on the ground.

When Grandmother and Jonny were seated on the blanket, she started to tell Jonny what had happened to this strange looking area.

"It was spring, and warm weather had returned to the north woods. Here, deep in the forest, above the smaller pines, birches, and oaks towered a huge, long-needled, white pine tree – this pine tree," Grandmother said as she touched the smooth gray wood of the tree.

"The year's growth of needles stretched upward toward the sun, which showered its warmth down onto the forest. The winter snow had melted early and the refreshing water was quickly drawn up into all the trees and plants. The plants and trees were very thirsty after a long winter sleep and they drank up the water greedily. They could sip the water up through their roots, and the pine tree needed more water then all the rest because it was so big. The soft, warm, southern breeze carried the birds into the woods. The birds began building their nests in the huge pine tree. They built their nest from dried grasses and pine needles that covered the ground after the winter. Their happy voices called to one another, bringing the sound of life back into the forest after the long winter.

"The pine tree had been a nesting place for hundreds of birds over the years. The squirrels and chipmunks lunched from the plump pine cones that dripped from the ends of the pine tree branches. All winter long they snacked on the pine cones and the ground was cluttered with broken remains. A mother deer had pawed out a bed in the earth under the pine tree. That indention is the bed the mother deer made for her family," Grandmother said as she pointed to a spot next to the blanket.

"It was spring and life was returning to the forest.

The spring brought others to the woods as well. Two fishermen were excited because winter was over and they were anxious to catch fish from the crystal clear river waters. The river was located not far from the huge pine tree. So, the two men decided to camp by the big pine tree. After many hours of fishing, the men decided to make something to eat. The fishermen had a small grill in which they started a fire to cook their dinner. After they started the grill fire, they walked back down to the river to clean the fish they had caught that day.

"While the men were cleaning the fish at the river, the gentle spring breeze changed. A strong gust of wind rushed through the trees and blew over the grill. The glowing coals spilled over the ground. The wind fanned the fire and quickly it spread over the dried out grasses, twigs, and pine needles that covered the ground. Rapidly the fire ran along the floor of the forest. With terrible speed, it leapt onto the trees and climbed through the dead leaves and dried branches. When the fishermen came back from cleaning the fish, they stood frozen in shock. They watched the fire jump from one dry pine tree branch to the next, climbing its way to the top of the huge pine tree with amazing speed. As the fire grew in size, it moved faster and faster, jumping from treetop to treetop. The men tried to stop the fire but soon they realized they must get out of the forest and get help. The fire ran through the forest, destroying the trees, plants, chasing away the birds and animals.

"The fire burned all that day and the next, finally it was stopped by a lake. But, it had destroyed everything in this area.

"When I arrived at this spot a few days after the fire, Jonny, all that was standing was the old pine tree. Everything was burned to the ground and everything was black and covered in ashes.

"Soon after the fire, the spring rains came and washed the black burned ashes into the ground and quickly new plants started to grow. The next summer the new bushes were thick with blueberries. I could pick them by the handfuls.

"But, it was a sad place. The birds didn't come back to build their nests in a tree with no branches for protection and no insects for food. The animals were afraid to come into an area where they could be seen so easily.

"Last year when I came to pick blueberries the bushes were again filled with wonderful round, fat, sweet tasting berries. The burned ashes from all the plants and trees gave new energy to the plants and berries. So, something good had come from this terrible fire. And the pine tree was no longer alone. High on the very top of the tree where a few broken branches still remained, a pair of osprey had built a huge nest – the nest you see up on top of the pine tree, Jonny. The osprey build their nest out of sticks and fill the inside with their own feathers. I'm surprised the osprey is not here now, chirping at us. They don't like people around their nesting area. When the osprey find a nesting place they like, they usually come back to the same nest every year. I know where the osprey is, it must be fishing!

"What do you mean fishing, Grandmother?" Jonny asked

"The osprey is a fish hawk," Grandmother continued, "all they eat are fish.

They fly high in the sky with their huge brown and white wings spread wide and glide over the lakes and streams. When they see a fish near the surface of the water they dive feet first into the water and grab the fish with their talons. Their talons are different from other birds. They have spike-like scales on the bottom of their feet. The sharp spikes help them to hold on to the slippery fish. Sometimes they catch a fish that is so big the osprey can hardly fly and carry the fish at the same time."

"Oh, Jonny, we are lucky!" Grandmother smiled. "Do you hear that loud chirping sound? That is the osprey returning.""

"Jonny listened and turned his head to look for the osprey. High above the pine tree he saw a big bird floating with its wings spread wide. Back and forth across the sky the bird floated. But the osprey would not land on the nest in the pine tree. "The people who take care of the forest protect the osprey from people who might want to harm them. We are not allowed to stay here and disturb the birds. I think we better check the blueberry bushes for blossoms and leave. The osprey must be doing repairs on their nest, so we must leave them to their work," Grandmother said as she stood up and folded the blanket.

Grandmother walked over to the small green bushes that covered the ground. "Come over here, Jonny," she called happily, "The blueberries will be good again this year. The bushes are covered with blossoms."

Jonny ran to where his grandmother was kneeling. When he knelt down closer to the bushes he saw the small white flowers covering the ends of the bushes. "They are really tiny, aren't they, Grandmother?"

"Yes, Jonny but each flower will be a berry. Blueberry picking will be good again this year."

When they reached the car, Jonny turned around and watched as the osprey glided slowly around in the sky getting closer to the pine tree. Finally the osprey dropped softly onto the edge of the nest. The two-foot tall osprey turned its head and loudly chirped, calling its mate. A few seconds passed and suddenly another osprey dropped onto the nest. "Boy! is the osprey ever a big bird!" Jonny said with his eyes opened wide."Look Grandmother, the mother and father osprey are both standing on the nest."

"Isn't it a wonderful sight when life has returned to the forest."

The Fall Train Trip

Every day seemed to be a new adventure.

Grandmother and Jonny Lump-Lump had spent the spring smelting and the summer fishing and collecting treasures. Later in the summer Grandmother and Jonny filled the freezer with all the vegetables that had grown in her garden. Throughout the whole summer berries were ready to pick and make into jams and jellies. They started in June picking strawberries, in July they picked the blueberries that grew wild in the forest, and later came the raspberry in grandmother's garden. Now was hazelnut picking time and the bushes were loaded with nuts. Every day Jonny learned something new from his grandmother. Some of the jobs were hard work, but they always had fun.

This was the first time he had stayed with his grandmother by the lake in the autumn. The forest looked like someone had dumped cans of paint all over the trees. The woods and hills were covered in red, yellow, gold, orange, and even pink colors. "The Lake Superior area is really beautiful in the fall," Jonny thought.

Grandmother said, "We used to say that Mother Nature was giving us a special gift in the fall. Mother Nature loaded the trees with fruits and nuts and painted the leaves with all the bright colors. It seemed nature's way of preparing us for the cold, colorless winter to come. A long winter when we must eat the food we've stored away, just like the animals and the native people who lived here years ago."

"What did the people do years ago when they didn't have freezers?" Jonny asked.

"They would cut huge blocks of ice out of the lake in the winter, and this ice kept things cold through out the year. The ice blocks became quite a big business when people didn't have refrigerators and freezers. But, my mother and father dug a deep hole in the ground and lined the hole with wood;

they called it a root cellar. There they stored potatoes and fruits and all canned goods safe from freezing. The native peoples who lived around the lake-harvested wild rice in the fall, as well as the fruits and berries. They would dry the fish they caught, the meat they trapped, the berries they picked, and wild rice harvested. They shared their knowledge about the animals and plants with the newcomers – showing them how to do the drying process – but my family liked the food that was canned better. There were lots of deer and bear and other animals for meat, but winter has always been a difficult time around Lake Superior because it is so cold and snowy.

"My grandfather moved here from the 'old country' where he had been a fisherman. He and many of his friends found a good life here. There were animals for meat, and fish to catch and sell, and lots of trees to cut into lumber for homes and (also) to sell." Grandmother continued.

"Soon after my grandfather arrived they found there was something very valuable under the ground as well. They found a mineral called iron ore. Soon many men and their families came from all over the world to help dig the iron ore out of the ground. They needed a way to move the heavy iron ore from where they dug it to where they made it into steel. They needed a railroad. Many more men were needed to build the railroad lines. The railroad tracks soon covered the whole area and the iron ore was hauled to the lake where the ore boats took the iron ore away. The men who dug the iron ore had good jobs and many of the men and women worked for the railroad, and still do today. Have you ever ridden on a train, Jonny?" Grandmother asked.

"No," he replied, "never!"

"Well, today we'll take a ride all along the lake and go to one of the places where the boats still pick up the iron ore. Would you like that?" She asked.

"Let's go, Grandmother!" Jonny called as he ran to get his jacket.

When they arrived at the train depot Jonny found it very interesting because the building was filled with all kinds of trains. He and Grand-mother walked through every train. It was a train museum.

Soon the train was ready to leave and their trip along the shoreline of Lake Superior began. Jonny was very excited because he had never ridden on a train before. Slowly they pulled out of the depot area and started up along the lake. As they came around a big bend in the track Jonny recognized something.

"Look Grandmother," he said as he pointed out the window, "there is Agate Beach where we found my special agate."

"That's right, Jonny. Look at the trees along the lake; they are unusually beautiful and full of color this year," Grandmother said, "This was a perfect day to come on our trip."

The train slowly traveled right along the shore of the lake. They traveled through some small villages. Grandmother explained these villages were once the places where the fishermen and their families lived. Her grandparents had known some of these families over a hundred years ago. Many of the families made their living cutting trees for the lumber companies or working on the railroad, as well as fishing.

When they arrived at the end of the railroad line the conductor told them they could walk over to the area where the boats were loaded with iron ore. He warned them that when the whistle blew the train would leave at 2:00p.m. "So don't be late." he warned again.

Grandmother had packed a nice lunch of strawberry and peanut butter sandwiches and lemonade. They sat at a picnic table in a small park by the lake.

Across from the park was the dock where the one-mile-long iron ore boat was being filled with iron ore. Grandmother took a photograph of Jonny standing in front of the boat so he could later share his adventure with his parents.

After their picnic lunch they walked back to the train and arrived just as the conductor blew the whistle.

Jonny Lump-Lump and Grandmother quickly climbed on board and found their seats. The ride back to the depot seemed to go by very quickly and as the train started to slow down Jonny turned to his grandmother and said, "I wish we could ride the train all the way around Lake Superior and see everything there is to see. Wouldn't that be wonderful. I bet there are all kinds of things we could learn."

"That would be wonderful!"
Grandmother agreed.

Tales of Lake Superior

ABOUT THE AUTHOR

Juliet Beatrice Niemi Lind was born and raised along the shores of Lake Superior. After fifty years of marriage, rearing a family, and traveling the world, her love and respect for the Lake Superior region has grown into a passion she hopes to share with others in the creative way of story telling. Juliet and her husband Ralph live in the northwoods not far from Lake Superior.

Text © 2011 by Juliet Beatrice Lind

First published by Joan Henrik Design, *Duluth, Minnesota*
First United States edition 2011

Proofers: *Billie Lange*
　　　　　Daniel Johnson

Printed in the United States
ISBN 978-0-615-54596-7